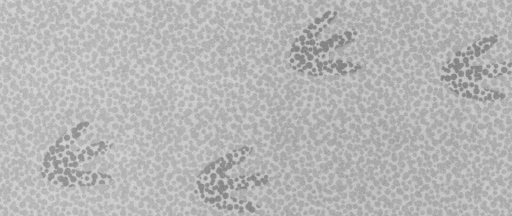

DINOFOURS®
Color-Word Storybook
PUPPET PLAY

by Steve Metzger
Illustrated by Hans Wilhelm

SCHOLASTIC INC.
New York   Toronto   London   Auckland   Sydney
Mexico City   New Delhi   Hong Kong   Buenos Aires

To Norman Finegold
—S.M.

Go to www.scholastic.com for Web site information on Scholastic authors and illustrators.

Text copyright © 2001 by Scholastic Inc.
Illustrations copyright © 2001 by Hans Wilhelm, Inc.
All rights reserved. Published by Scholastic Inc.
SCHOLASTIC, DINOFOURS, and associated logos are trademarks and/or registered trademarks of Scholastic Inc.

ISBN 0-439-32048-8

12 11 10 9 8 7 6 5 4 3 2 1   01 02 03 04 05

Printed in the U.S.A.
First Scholastic printing, November 2001

Help Your Child Learn to Read with Dinofours® Color-Word Storybooks

On this page, you'll find a list of several words in color. Point to the first color word (the word "**puppet**") as you read it to your child. Let your child know that the word "**puppet**" will be red every time it appears in this book. Then have your child repeat the word "**puppet**" back to you. As you read the story, point out each color word to your child.

The first time you read the story, you might want to read it through without using the color-word feature. The second time, you might want to ask your child to read just one of the color words. As your child gains confidence, he or she might want to read a second color word...then a third...then a fourth. It's all up to you and your child!

The color words for this book are:

puppet/puppets   dance/danced

show/shows   sing/sang

Circle Time had just ended, and the Dinofours were ready for their next activity.

"We're going to make paper bag **puppets** today," Mrs. Dee said. "Does that sound like fun?"

"Yes!" the children replied.

"I *love* making **puppets**!" Tara said. "It's my favorite thing to do."

"That's great," said Mrs. Dee.

"Can we have a **puppet** show when we're done?" asked Tara. "I love **puppet** shows!"

"That's a fine idea!" said Mrs. Dee. "Now, let's get started."

The Dinofours scampered over to the art table and quickly found chairs to sit on. Danielle and Tracy made sure they were sitting next to each other.

There were all kinds of **puppet**-making materials on the table. The children found buttons, colored paper scraps, cotton balls, sheets of newspaper, paper towel rolls, and pieces of fabric and yarn waiting for them.

"What are these for?" asked Danielle, holding up a paper bag.

"Those are the paper bags that you'll be using to make your **puppets**," said Mrs. Dee. "The first thing to do is to open them up."

Brendan took his paper bag and put it over his head.

"Look at me!" he called out. "I'm a ghost. *Wooooo!*"

"Brendan," said Mrs. Dee. "Please take that bag off your head and listen."

"All right, Mrs. Dee," Brendan said. He took the paper bag off his head and put it on the table.

Mrs. Dee told the children how to make their **puppets**. When she finished, the Dinofours quickly got to work.

"My **puppet** is going to have lots of pretty hair," Tracy said as she lifted up a bunch of yarn. "She's going to be a singing **puppet**."

"Mine will be a flying **puppet**," Albert said as he glued on two buttons for his **puppet's** eyes.

"My **puppet** will be a swimmer," said Danielle. "She's not afraid of the water."

"And mine will be a monster **puppet**," Brendan said. "He's going to scare all the other **puppets**."

"He's not going to scare *my* **puppet**," said Joshua. "My **puppet** will be a superhero **puppet** with special powers. What about your **puppet**, Tara?" he asked. "You haven't said anything."

"My **puppet** is going to be a dancing **puppet**," Tara said as she drew a big smile on her **puppet's** face. "She's the best dancer in the world. And she really wants to dance with the other **puppets** when we have our **puppet** show."

The children happily made their **puppets**. When they finished, Mrs. Dee put the **puppets** on a nearby shelf.

"Can we have our **puppet show** now?" Tara asked.

"Not yet," Mrs. Dee replied. "We have to wait for the glue to dry. That should be when Snack Time is over."

"I can't wait!" Tara said.

During Snack Time, Tara was so excited thinking about the **puppet** show that she only ate one Dino Cracker.

Then Tara sang this song:

> My **puppet** loves to dance, dance, DANCE!
> That's what she loves to do.
> And when we have our **puppet** show,
> She'll do a dance for you!

When Snack Time ended, Mrs. Dee brought out a large, empty cardboard box and put it down on the rug.

"This box will be the **puppet** stage," said Mrs. Dee. Then she gave the children their **puppets**.

"*Boo!*" Brendan's **puppet** said to Tracy's **puppet**.

"My **puppet** is not scared of your **puppet**," Tracy said. "Now tell your **puppet** to go away."

Brendan put his **puppet** on his lap.

"Will everyone please sit in front of the box so you can see?" Mrs. Dee asked. As the children moved into place, Mrs. Dee asked Tara to go first.

"Okay," Tara said as she sat behind the box. "Who wants to **dance** with my **puppet**?"

Nobody answered.

Finally, Albert spoke. "My **puppet** can't dance with your **puppet** because mine's a flying **puppet**." Albert zoomed his **puppet** through the air. "See?"

"My **puppet** is a swimming **puppet**," said Danielle as she pretended that her **puppet** was swimming. "She can't dance."

"Monster **puppets** are too scary to dance," Brendan said.

"And my **puppet** can only sing," said Tracy. She lifted up her **puppet** and made it sing, "La, la, la."

Tara got madder and madder as she listened to her classmates.

"I don't like you anymore!" Tara shouted as she stomped off to her cubby. "And I don't like your silly **puppets**, either!" Then Tara began to cry.

Mrs. Dee walked over and tried to comfort Tara.

A little while later, Joshua stood up and walked over to Tara, too.

"Tara, I haven't told you about *my* **puppet**," Joshua said.

Tara lifted her head to listen.

"Even though my **puppet** has super powers," Joshua continued, "he still likes to **dance**. Can my **puppet** **dance** with your **puppet**?"

Tara stopped crying. "Yes," she said.

"I guess my **puppet** can do a swimming dance," said Danielle joining in.

"My **puppet** can do a flying dance," Albert added.

"Mine can do a scary dance," said Brendan.

"And mine can dance and sing at the same time!" Tracy said. Turning to Tara, she asked, "Can *all* of our **puppets** be in your show?"

"Sure!" said Tara with a great, big smile. Then the Dinofours and Mrs. Dee walked back over to the **puppet** stage. All of the children joined Tara behind the box.

"Now who's going to *watch* the show?" asked Danielle. "All of the children are here."

"I will!" said Mrs. Dee, sitting down. "I can hardly wait!"

"Okay," said Tara. "Let the **show** begin!"

The **puppets** **danced** and swam and flew and **sang**.

When the **show** ended, Mrs. Dee clapped and clapped.

The children's **puppets** bowed...again and again.

"That was the best **puppet** **show** ever!" Mrs. Dee said.

Then Tara **sang** a new song:

*Dancing **puppets**, singing **puppets**,*
***Puppets** in a row.*
*Flying **puppets**, swimming **puppets** —*
*What a **puppet** show!*

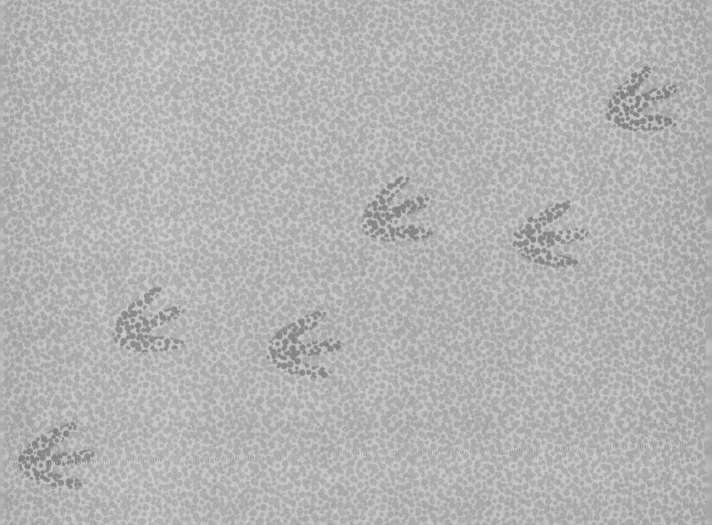

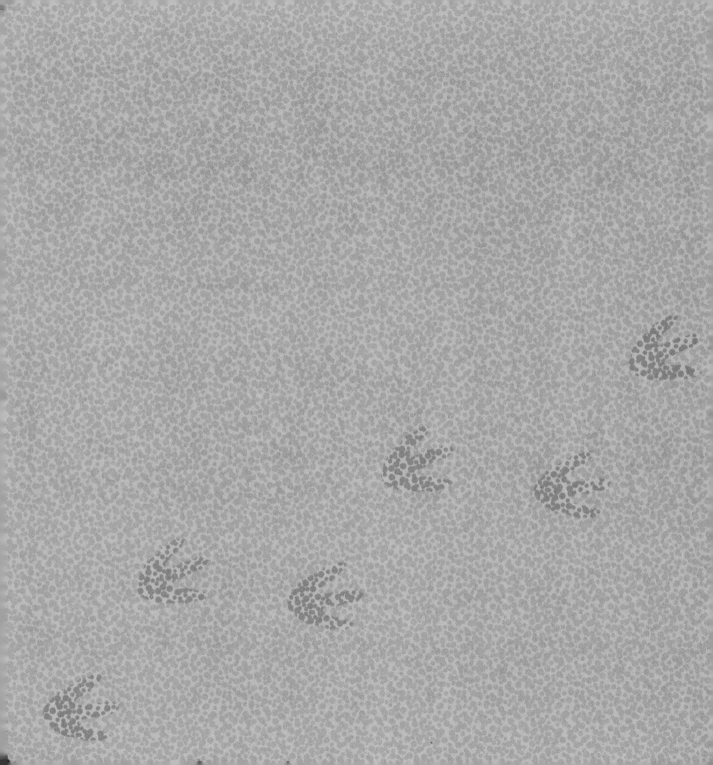